CW00869168

For Cara and Lochlann
Written with Love,
By Mummy.

ISBN Number 978-1-8381605-0-0

www.mummyclifford.com
nuala@mummyclifford.com

Hello! My name is Lochlann,
and I am a new baby.
I have bright red hair and
a big, happy smile.

I also have a big sister.

Everyone tells me how lucky
I am to have my big sister.

But when mummy and daddy weren't looking, sometimes she was mean to me.

She pulled my hair...

Big Sister,
don't be **BOLD!**

She bit my toe...

Big Sister, don't be BOLD!

She hid
my bottle...

Big Sister,
don't be
BOLD!

She didn't want to share her toys and worse, she didn't want to share her mummy!

She really was
very mean to me.

Now a little bit of time has passed and I think my big sister has got used to me...

Now she brushes my hair...

My big sister is a
Good big sister!

Now she feeds
me my bottle...

My big sister is a
VERY GOOD
big sister!

B
B
A
C

Now she brings me my toys...

My big sister is the **best big sister** in the whole wide world

Now she loves me so much she doesn't want to share me.

I really love my big sister and I know she really loves me!

About the Author

Nuala Boyle aka Mummy Clifford

Nuala became a mother to Cara at the age of 39 and then to Lochlann at the age of 41. As a mother to two very young children who never slept, Nuala spent night after night walking the hallways of her home trying to nurse her babies to sleep. Whilst she was pacing, she reflected on delightful and often humorous incidents that had happened that day and she decided to write them down. From these scribbles, the Don't Be Bold series of uplifting children's stories emerged.

The Don't Be Bold series of books are Nuala's first venture into the world of children's publications, but she is not new to writing. Nuala's career is in education management and whilst she is more used to writing reports, service guides, student handbooks, penning responses to ministers' questions and writing press releases, she finds authoring children's stories a delightful diversion and is keen to explore where it might take her.

About the Illustrator

Roisin Bradley

Roisin is a Belfast-based illustrator and graphic designer. She graduated in 2000 from Falmouth College of Arts with a degree in illustration. She has had four children's picture books published, one of which, 'Samson's Titanic Journey' was a top three best seller. It is now part of the NI Curriculum and is used to teach children about the history of the Titanic.

Working with a wide range of clients, she has used many styles; from realistic watercolours to create animated medical illustrations, to black and white illustrations full of characters straight from her imagination. This series is Roisin's first digitally-drawn set of illustrations, created completely on the iPad. You can find her work at roisinbradley.weebly.com

She dedicates this book to her daughter Emer, who shares her passion for art and illustration.

Nuala and Roisin are currently working on new books in this series including:

Don't Be Bold - The story of a Bold Daddy
Don't Be Bold - My Granny's NOT Bold
Don't Be Bold - The story of a Bold Doggy

They very much look forward to sharing them with you!

Lightning Source UK Ltd.
Milton Keynes UK
UKHW050243301120
374206UK00014B/37